IT STARTED WITH THE WITCH'S SPELL

A ZOEY AND ARTHUR ADVENTURE

It Started With the Witch's Spell

Eight-year-old Zoey loves adventures and princesses. She and her mother have read every princess story that they can find. Arthur hates princesses; he loves dinosaurs. He's not sure about adventures. He is all boy, or is he?

It's summer in Zoey's new town. She has no friends yet. She finds she has a lot of time but nothing to do. Zoey's new next-door neighbor, Mrs. Gianopolopolous, Mrs. G to her friends, helps with both problems.

Soon, with the help of Mrs. G, Zoey meets Arthur and the two of them find themselves in the middle of a well-known princess story. There, Zoey and Arthur meet a princess with a terrifying problem. But, with equal parts courage and kindness, and by listening to everyone, Zoey proves that kids can have amazing adventures and solve big problems too.

THIS BOOK BELONGS TO:

_____

IT STARTED WITH HE WITCH'S SPELL

A ZOEY AND ARTHUR ADVENTURE

By Joanna Hurley

Illustrations by Anca Chelaru

To my beloved Bryan, who believed in me and supported me before anyone else knew that I could write.

Author's Message

My hope for my readers is that each of you grows up loving to read. I want your early reading adventures with Zoey and Arthur to be lots of fun and help you learn to be strong and confident so that all of your dreams can come true.

Acknowledgements

A big, big thanks to my dear family and friends for your help on this book journey. It is not always fun to read drafts, look at photos, and everything in between. I truly appreciate all of your efforts. That means you: Trish O'Farrell, Lin May, Penny Loiez, Bob Hurley, Kathleen Hurley, reading specialist extraordinaire, Claire McDonald, Ann Phaum, Paul Baines, Mary Jane Fry, Michel Fernandez, Jany Rey, and Margaret Hinski. I also would be remiss not to thank my publisher, Divya Parekh, and her team for always going the extra mile to ensure that my book is given every opportunity from a production and marketing basis to be a huge success. You are all excellent at what you do, and it is genuinely appreciated.

Contents

Illustrations

Chapter 1
The Move

"Good grief, Arthur, I'm so tired of you complaining about Mrs. G and the spell she put on you!"

Who's Arthur?

Who's Mrs. G?

Did she really put a spell on Arthur?

I will tell you everything, but I'd better start at the beginning. It's a bit of a long story. My name is Zoey. I am eight years old.

"We're moving to a new house," Mom announced one day last month.

I really would have preferred living at Grandma's house. I loved it there. But while I always want things my way, this time, I figured I had to do what my parents wanted. So, I didn't yell or even have a tantrum! So much for growing up.

After "THE ANNOUNCEMENT," as Dad called it, there was a constant hustle and bustle in our family. It continued until we finally arrived at the new house.

"Zoey, collect your toys and animals in this box. I will pack your clothes in that blue suitcase. Your father will use the brown one, and I will use that funny old pink one for my clothes."

During our pre-move frenzy, Dad labored over a list of all the things we would take to the new house. An "inventory," he called it. He popped in and out of my room with questions every few minutes.

"Are we taking the old dresser from Grandma?"

"Yes, Dad. Mom says we are taking everything in my room but my old bed. She says we're buying a new bed for my room."

After weeks of work, we filled the house with boxes. Then the questions started. My parents asked each other questions. They asked me questions. They called people and asked them questions. There were more questions than I had ever heard in my whole life.

I wasn't sure if all these questions would result in the 'smooth move' Mom said she wanted. I didn't even know what a 'smooth move' meant. I just wanted to be done with the packing and the questions and for us to get to the new house. I wanted to see if it would be as much fun as my grandparents' house. But I wasn't so sure it could be.

"Where's the rest of my sandwich? I only took a bite."

"Where does that go?"

"Do you want to take this?"

"Who put that in this box?"

2

Finally, we arranged our winter clothes in boxes and our summer clothes in suitcases. Big men, sort of giants, with black belts around their waists, transformed our furniture into plastic-wrapped presents. Everything else was boxed, labeled, and loaded onto the big moving truck.

The new house was far from our old home, about 4 hours away. We had an incredible drive traveling there. We sang songs from the radio and played a guessing game about the things we noticed along the road. I was having so much fun that I forgot about missing Grandma and my old friends. It was fun to be a traveling family, and maybe the new house would be wonderful too.

When we got to Treetown, it was late afternoon. I gazed with interest at everything. The new town was larger than Grandma's village, where we had lived the last few years. I guess it was about the same size as the town where we had lived before. Well, maybe the new town is a bit bigger. I don't know for sure how many people live there.

There is a welcome sign at the edge of the town. A car crashed into it, and so it hangs on a funny angle with the bottom half of the sign missing. Now it says, "WELCOME TO." Maybe the sign never said how many people lived in the town. Maybe it's an old sign and would have had the wrong number of people on it. Maybe it... I could go on and on. I am a "maybe" person. My mom calls that imagination. My dad says it's sort of annoying.

Treetown is the same as any other town, I guess, but with lots of trees. It has churches, grocery stores, a movie theatre, schools, and a candy store. Mom says that it's a penny candy store. Not sure, but I hope so. Anyways, the candy store is the best part of Treetown. I'm not sure about my new school. It's summer, and I haven't been there yet.

My parents purchased a new house for us in Treetown. I like our new home. It's red brick and has a big front porch. You can drink lemonade on the porch after you have finished your chores. After dinner, it's the place where we sit to eat chocolate cake. The backyard has flowers and a playset. The swings are great, but I really, really enjoy all the flowers. My mom cuts them and puts them in vases all around the house. I get some for my bedroom too. She says they make the place feel homey. I adore the colors. There are red, purple, yellow, and orange flowers; almost an entire box of crayons right in your garden. The rest of the house is okay.

My bedroom is definitely average. It's not too large or too small. It has windows so you can see things in the room even when the lights aren't on. Mom and Dad let me pick my favorite colors for the paint. Blue and white. Yep. It was pink before.

I know some girls love pink, but that's just not me. I am pretty simple. I love my grandparents, princesses, animals, adventures, and every dessert ever baked. Cookies, cakes and brownies, everything! Oops. I love my parents too even though I am still mad at my mom about making us move.

My bedroom is nice now. I keep all my things in my room: my clothes, Bingly, my stuffed bear, and my toys. I have a desk in my room too. I will do my schoolwork there when school finally starts in September.

As she leaned down for a goodnight kiss, Mom announced, "I know the house is crammed full of boxes, but I think tomorrow we should go to town. First, we need to locate a store to buy you a bed."

"I don't mind camping on the floor," I smiled, "but if you want to go, that sounds fine to me."

The following day, the three of us headed to the center of town. We discovered a big clothing store, a hardware store, a big grocery store, and finally a store that advertised beds. We parked and went into Gary's Bed Emporium.

A tall, balding man came up to us with a big smile. "Hi ya folks. What brings you in today?"

He looked like a guy from a TV ad but otherwise was okay.

"We're looking for a new bed for our daughter, Zoey. We just moved to town yesterday," my dad said.

"Well, welcome. Welcome to Treetown. I've lived here all my life, and I still love it here. When do you need the bed delivered?"

"Zoey is camping on her bedroom floor at the moment, so we want it delivered as soon as possible," Mom said.

We searched the store for hours. The beds were not exciting. I had an old iron bed at Grandma's house with metal flowers across the back I loved. Here the beds were all wood or a plastic-looking material. I climbed up on so many beds I should have been a bed tester. I had a strong urge to jump up and down on the beds to test them. That sounded like fun. My mom looked over at me. Her look stopped me in my tracks. How do Moms always know what we are thinking?

I finally picked a bed, but it was pretty dull. My parents wanted me to have a bed. Any bed. I know I was supposed to be excited about the new bed, but I wasn't. I had a perfect bed at Grandma's house going to waste.

I know you're probably wondering, what happened to Arthur?

You will understand when you meet Arthur, but first things first. You need to meet Mrs. G, as she is important too.

KidQuest: Have you ever moved to a new town? This move has been hard on Zoey. She misses her grandparents. I think she doesn't know if she can be as happy living someplace new without them. What do you think? Was your move hard too?

Well, let's get back to the story now.

Chapter 2
The Spell

Mrs. G is our next-door neighbor. I call her Mrs. G, but her real name is Mrs. Gianopolopolous. Some people in our neighborhood think she's a bit odd - a witch even - but not me. They just don't know her. I will admit that she is very short and has funny red hair and an odd smile and is missing some of her teeth. Wow! When I think of it, she's the spitting image of me! All I know is that she's thoughtful, friendly, and well, bewitching.

When we lived with Grandma and Grandpa, I didn't have a lot of friends. I didn't need them as I loved having fun with my grandparents. Grandma taught me how to cook, and Grandpa let me help with the animals on their farm. He keeps goats, horses, pigs, and cows. I love them, especially Percival, the baby pig.

I want to be with fun people. I'm not sure if they need to be friends or if a family is enough. But without my grandparents, maybe I will want some friends. For now, Mrs. G is my only friend in Treetown.

I met Mrs. G the day we moved in. She brought cookies to our house to welcome us to the neighborhood. Delicious oatmeal cookies, full of bananas and raisins! I can make friends quickly sometimes. Just give me some good cookies, and I am your friend for life. Otherwise, it takes me a while to make friends.

A few weeks after the move, while my parents were still going through boxes and deciding where to put things, Mrs. G suggested I come over. I think it was to get me out of their way. That sounded good to me. I had worked hard to set up my room Now I was getting a bit tired of being told to put things away in the rest of the house.

All I heard was, "Put this here."

"No there."

"No, put it back. It's better there."

Yuk! I needed a vacation from the unpacking. Even if only for a day.

So, I went over, and Mrs. G showed me her house and garden Inside the house, strange things hung from the ceiling that sort of looked like onions. There were also some bottles with odd and scary-looking things inside. The garden startled me too. A big black pot stood over a wood fire. Mrs. G showed me how to stir it. As I stirred, Mrs. G showed me some herbs growing in her garden. I guessed that the strange green potion in the pot had herbs in it, too. While stirring the pot, I told Mrs. G about my bed.

"I have to sleep in it all night, and it's boring. It's just a big wooden bed." I confessed. "While it's new, it just isn't as nice as my iron bed at Grandma's house."

"Why did you leave your Grandma's house?"

"Well, Grandma got sick for a while. So, we hurried there to help and lived with her and Grandpa for a few years. I love my grandmother, and so I treasured being with her. On her good days, she taught me how to make cookies and cakes and other good things. Grandpa is nice too. He is not too talky, but he makes great kites and good pancakes on the weekends. They live in a small village in the countryside in a big old house. The village has lots of frogs, dogs, donkeys, and sometimes horses and cows. I love their village.

"Finally, Grandma got better. We baked a cake to celebrate. I almost cried that day; I was so happy. I hated it when Grandma was weak and had to be helped all the time. Usually, she's a warrior. Me too, my dad says. Then my mom decided we should get our own house and ruined everything. I wanted things to stay the same."

"It was nice that you all helped your grandmother. I bet she was pretty happy you were there."

"Yep. She adored us being there."

"You didn't begrudge having to help her so much?"

12

"No, I love her."

She glanced over at me. Then looked away as if in thought. Then she peeked back at me. She was plotting something. I was sure of it.

"Since you were so nice to your Grandma, maybe I can do something for you."

Then, winking at me, she said, "I think that I can fix your bed problem! Do you think that you would have wanted a big brother or an older cousin?"

"Sure!"

"Well, let's see what I can do."

A little while later, we returned to my house. We ate some cookies with Mom and then I showed Mrs. G my bedroom. Suddenly, as we stood by my bed, she recited some funny words over and over again.

"Bits and bats, and bits and bobs, bedaboop, bedabip, bedabing, beds who listen have fun! Come to life. Come to life. Learn to speak!"

I was amazed at what Mrs. G said. Well, we would see what happened. Then she went home, and I had lunch.

After lunch, Mom decided that I should take a nap. I hadn't been feeling well the day before, and she thought I looked tired. I agreed I was a bit tired and that it was probably a good idea. So, went to my room and laid down on my bed.

Suddenly, the bed shook, and someone bellowed, "Hey!"

Who was in my bedroom? I knew that it wasn't my mom or dad. It wasn't one of their voices I heard. The voice came from my bed. I looked under it. No one was there. Not seeing anyone, I went ahead and took my nap.

KidQuest: Do you believe in spells and magic? Want me to turn you into a frog? A rabbit? A cow? A spider? Even if I want to turn you into something?

Now, let's get back to the story.

Chapter 3
Arthur

When I woke up, my stuffed bear, Bingly, and my other toys were strewn all over. Bewildered, I examined my room to see if anything else had changed. I soon realized that my bed looked different too. Was that possible? Well, it was ! I just knew it. A red baseball cap was hanging on the bedpost, and the cap had a big "A" on it. I knew it wasn't mine. I'd never seen it before. So, what had happened while I was sleeping? Soon, I knew.

"What were those stuffed animals and toys doing all over me?" a voice yelled.

I frowned. Then my mouth shot open in disbelief. While I could not understand it, the voice again was coming from my bed. My bed has a design in the middle of the headboard, and the voice came from there.

I didn't think. I just responded, "The toys and animals are mine, and I keep them on MY bed!" I yelled back.

"Well, don't get angry. The toys are heavy, you know, and you're getting heavier every day too!"

I changed the topic, "When did you learn to speak?"

The bed nodded at me, "How could I play with you if I couldn't talk? I don't know how it happened, but I can speak now. I don't think that I could until today."

We eyed each other. "Let's play now then!" I laughed.

The bed looked at me and said, "I can only play with you at nap time and night."

I nodded. "Okay, then I'll see you later. By the way, what's your name? You do have a name, don't you?"

The bed stood quite still for a few minutes and then said, "My name is... My name is... Arthur."

KidQuest: Has your bed ever yelled at you as Arthur yelled at Zoey? What language do you think beds speak?

Ready to go back to the story?

Chapter 4
The Adventure Begins

That night, when Mom said it was bedtime, I said goodnight quickly. No delaying. After all, I was curious to see just how Arthur would be able to play with me. I put on the princess nightgown my mom bought me and snuggled under the covers. After I finished my prayers, Mom and I read my favorite story, then she turned off my bedroom light and went downstairs.

Pretty soon, a voice whispered, "Are we alone?"

"Yes, Arthur, we are. So, what are we going to play? Where are we going?"

Arthur knew precisely what he wanted to do, "I want to go to a zoo or a museum!"

"No, Arthur, I want to visit a fairyland and meet a real princess. That's what we should do!"

"No, No, No!" Arthur wailed, "I have to stay in this house all day while you go out and play. It was better before I could talk. Mrs. G shouldn't have put that spell on me. Now it's hard for me to lie around all day. I want to do normal kinds of kid things. I want to see the town!"

I shook my head, "No. I want to see a princess! What use is having a friend if they won't play what you want to play?" I hrieked.

Arthur was just as forceful as I was. "No, I'm not going to see ome prissy old princess!"

I put an end to the arguing, "You are MY BED, and you'll go vhere I say, and that's it!"

"Okay, missy, you win. We will go to a fairyland," Arthur onceded, and then we both laughed.

"So, how do we play together?" I said to Arthur.

"When you are under the covers, we can go on adventures."

I was already under the covers, and so I asked, "What now?"

"If you are quite ready, we shall begin," Arthur said in an odd nglish accent.

KidQuest: Are you bossy with your friends? By the way, do you now how Zoey and Arthur find a fairyland for their trip? I don't hink you can find one on a map. Would you want to go on the dventure with Zoey and Arthur? I would!

Back to the story now.

Chapter 5
The Castle

It was just a few minutes later when I opened my eyes. Then I rubbed them in shock. I could not believe what I saw. I was standing in front of a gigantic castle with a moat and lots of towers. In one tower window stood a princess. She was lovely. She had long blond hair and was wearing a blue dress. Her crown glistened in the sun. She was everything I had pictured a princess would be.

I scanned the countryside for Arthur. I thought Arthur would be by my side, but I couldn't see him anywhere. Where had he gotten to? My mom would have said he was not very responsible, but he is a bed! Oh well, I would just have to explore the castle by myself. I was the one who wanted to see a fairyland after all. As I walked toward the castle, it was late afternoon. I walked across a long wooden bridge through a gate. Then I followed some winding streets to a large wooden door.

When I passed through this second gate, I found that I was actually in the central part of the castle. The entrance was beautiful, with a large chandelier. Pictures of kings, queens, princesses, and princes peered down from the walls. A fire blazed in a cavernous stone fireplace; huge logs crackled and hissed. To the left, a long winding staircase rose upwards.

A strange feeling shot through me. I started up the stairs, mysteriously drawn by something up there. When I reached the top, I peeked into room after room. Each was beautiful with a large wooden bed, colorful rugs, and curtains in reds, blues, and yellows. Finally, I peeked into a room and gawked in amazement at what I saw. There was Arthur with about 20 mattresses on top of him!

KidQuest: Would you have gone into the castle to explore as Zoey did? Do you think she was courageous?

Back to the story.

Chapter 6
Princess Zoerinda

Lying on top of the mattresses was the princess I had seen in the tower window. She was sound asleep. Her long hair draped over the side of the bed. I tip-toed into the room and sat down on the floor by the edge of the bed. Oops, I mean, I sat down next to Arthur.

"Arthur, I thought you didn't come with me. I looked around everywhere for you. Where were you all this time?"

I admit that I was grumpy when asking this. I was relieved that Arthur was safe at the castle. It was our first adventure together, after all. I was looking forward to spending time with him. It was more complex than I had imagined having an adventure with a bed.

Arthur whispered, "Well, I am a BED, so I couldn't be out there walking with you in the countryside, could I?

Arthur had such a strong personality. I wasn't sure what he could do and couldn't do. I hadn't thought about the fact that Arthur couldn't play with me. He is a bed. I should have thought about that. Most of the time, I am smarter than that. He sounds like a cranky boy, so I forget he's a bed. I started to giggle, and soon we were both laughing.

At this point, a pretty face appeared, and then a body followed. It was the princess standing in front of me. Then she adjusted her gown and smiled a lovely smile at me.

"Thank you for calling on me. My name is Zoerinda. (Zōrinda). This is my castle. I am the Princess Du Lit (pronounce it "Doo Lee"). But you can call me Zoerinda.

"I met the prince of this kingdom when we were both very young. I lived in a house in the forest. He journeyed to the woods to hunt. Then he returned again and again until we fell in love. It was a special time for us.

"My parents died when I was young. My governess raised me. Jean, the Prince, introduced me to his family after we fell in love. His mother refused to believe that I was a princess in my kingdom. The Queen tested me for months to see if I was a real princess. Finally, she made me lie on this bed as the last test. I could not sleep, but somehow, I passed the test.

"Jean is not here. He went to war to fight our enemies. When he is gone, I always sleep on this old bed. It reminds me of when we met. His parents, the King and Queen, are very old. We will be the King and Queen here soon."

She frowned and admitted, "I am worried about the King and

28

Queen. They are frightened. I don't know why I am telling you any of this."

I grinned. " It may be because I am young and won't tell anyone. Also, I know how to listen."

She laughed, "Maybe. The King's sorcerer predicted that raiders would attack the castle. The prediction worries the King. The sorcerer foresaw the beat of many hooves and feet over the castle's old wooden moat bridge. The King sent for Jean, but we have no idea when to expect him. We also do not know when the attack will occur. It may be tomorrow, or it may be next year. It's very troubling. I don't want this to make the King or Queen sick."

"Wow! I didn't know that princesses could have problems. Are you sure that the sorcerer is right?"

"Well, the King says that the sorcerer has always been right in the past. Whether right or wrong, the King and Queen feel helpless."

"I'm worried. I haven't slept well for years, but now I hardly sleep at all."

"I'm so sorry. That's awful. Can I help?"

"No, my dear. It is kind of you to offer. But I can't think of anything a little girl can do. Even one dressed in a princess nightgown. It's impossible to do anything when we do not know when an attack will take place."

I sighed. I didn't know what to say to reassure the princess or what to do to make her kingdom safe. If I had read about her in a book, then I would have known what happened next. Then I would have been able to prevent the attack. Instead, we stood there a long time, both thinking, but neither of us had a solution.

She yawned. "I am sorry to be rude, but I need to go back to sleep" She climbed back onto Arthur. Soon the princess's snoring disturbed the otherwise quiet castle.

"The Princess is nice, but I've never heard of a Princess Du Lit in any of my princess books. I don't think she is telling us the truth. That story she told us is incredible!"

Arthur laughed, "I think she is telling the truth. She is a princess! I am sure of it. Princess Du Lit is not a funny name. It just means "princess of the bed" in French."

Arthur was smart, but I was not going to tell him that. Then he would be even bossier. I was feeling closer to Arthur, but he was still bossy, grumpy, and all boy. It would take a while to see if we became friends.

KidQuest: Did the Princess's story about the sorcerer surprise you? It did me. Do you know the difference between a sorcerer, wizard, warlock, and magician?

Let's see what happens next.

Chapter 7
The Berbers

I explored the castle while the princess slept. It was so much fun seeing everything that Mom and I read about in my storybooks. Every part of the castle was interesting. I saw the room which stored all the knights' armor, the banquet room, and even the kitchen. Finally, I returned to Arthur to say that maybe we should be going home. But, before we could decide, something happened that changed everything.

Suddenly, horse hooves thundered ominously over the moat bridge and into the castle. Then we heard men shouting. I looked out the princess's window. Men were running into the castle.

I turned to Arthur, "What do they want? Do you think that they're after the princess? Are these the men the sorcerer talked about?"

"I don't know, but we need to do something," Arthur said, sounding frightened.

I looked at him, a bit surprised. He had grown close to the princess in a short time. Arthur was much nicer in fairyland than at home. He was grumpy there. Here he liked people more, or at least he liked beautiful princesses.

I didn't think about it. But I knew that if anyone were going to save the Princess and the Kingdom, it would have to be me.

But should I try?

Could I help?

The princess said I was only a little girl and that I couldn't help. I was scared, but someone needed to do something.

I ran to the princess's bedroom door and locked it. Then I crawled out the window. There was a large ledge outside the princess's window. I crawled onto the ledge and soon reached the next bedroom. I climbed through the window and went downstairs.

The invaders were everywhere. Their long robes fluttered as they ran here and there. They were looking inside the castle's cabinets and under furniture. I decided they were looking for someone. Since I wasn't even supposed to be at the castle, I knew they couldn't be looking for me. I walked right up to the man that I thought was the leader.

"What are you doing here?" I demanded, trying not to shake or appear afraid.

He looked me up and down. I was still in my princess nightgown.

He inquired, "I might ask you the same thing, young lady. We

are here looking for Princess Du Lit. Are you a princess? Are you the Princess Du Lit?"

I held my shoulders high as my mom had taught me.

"No, I am not Princess Du Lit. I play princess all the time, but I am not a real princess. Princess Du Lit is not here. You should leave at once. You are trespassing. Only Princess Zoerinda lives here."

"Oh," the man sighed. "We have been looking for the Princess Du Lit for so long."

I was curious now. "Why are you looking for the Princess Du Lit?"

The man sat down on the bottom step of the castle's winding staircase. "My name is Saeed. I am the leader of the Berbers. Our people roam the world. We have no true home!"

Immediately, I felt terrible. Had I been rude? Homes are really important. I knew that from my own experience.

"You could buy new houses. My Mom and Dad bought a new house recently. My Mom and Dad worked with a man to find our new house. He could find you and your friends houses too!" I giggled, happy that I had found a solution.

"True," he said, "but we are on a quest to find a place that makes good beds."

I almost chuckled. I thought they were looking for good beds instead of grumpy ones like Arthur.

"But what does the Princess Du Lit have to do with your search for a new home?" I inquired.

"Well, we need a place that makes good beds, and she is a famous bed tester."

I contemplated his statement for a long time. Then, all at once, I believed that I understood.

"I think that you are confused," I announced. "My mom read me lots of stories about princesses. But none of the princesses had jobs. Especially not a job like a bed tester."

"Is your Mother wise?" he queried.

"Yes, yes she is. She knows everything about princesses!"

He looked down at me and my princess nightgown.

"I see. A princess in this kingdom sleeps on many mattresses. We assumed that she was testing them. We thought that she could test beds for us and tell us where we should make our home. We think that Princess Zoerinda is the Princess du Lit."

KidQuest: Would you have spoken to the Berber leader as Zoey did? Do you think Zoey was afraid? Would you have had the courage to help the princess? Finished thinking?

Let's get back to the story.

KidQuest: Do you know about the Berber people? They are people who live in the desert in North Africa and raise camels and other animals. They move from place to place, selling their animals and other things. Do you know where Africa is? I put a map to help you understand where it is.

Look at the map and then back to the story.

Chapter 8
The Princess and the Pea

Chuckling, I realized my mom HAD told me the story of *The Princess and the Pea*. I think that the princess in that story was who Saeed was thinking about. So, I started to retell the story to him.

"There was a young girl who met a handsome prince and claimed to be a princess. Her family died, and she lived with her governess. The prince's mother, the queen, was suspicious. She wanted to make sure that the girl was a real princess and not a fake. So, the queen decided to test the girl by putting a small pea under many mattresses. If the girl could feel the pea, she was a princess. Then, she could marry the prince."

"Oh." Then Saeed asked, "You mean the girl was being tested?

"Yes," I replied.

"Well, was she a princess?" he asked.

Nodding my head up and down, I replied, "Yes."

Kid Quest: Did you ever read the story of *The Princess and The Pea*? Do you think Saeed is looking for the princess in the story?

Let's get back to our story then and see what happens!

Chapter 9
Finding a Bedland

"Oh." Saeed groaned, "So, we've been traveling for so many years for nothing? Our quest has failed! Failed." He wailed. His men looked up in surprise and got out their long silvery sabers, ready to attack whatever had caused their leader's cry.

"Well, maybe not! I may know someone who can help you. I'm not sure. I'll be right back."

Saeed stared at me as I dashed up the winding staircase. I went back to the room next to the princess's bedroom. Then I climbed back into the princess's bedroom.

Arthur stirred a bit and yawned. "What's up?"

"I need to talk to you and the princess. Quick!"

Arthur shook himself, and soon he and the princess were both wide awake. I asked them my questions.

"Do either of you consider yourself an expert on beds? I mean, do you know where the best beds are made?"

"Well," admitted the princess, "I know where the most comfortable beds are made. I have slept on mattresses from many lands, but the best beds are from Morocco. They have

ovely pine and oak trees there to build bed frames. They also have good mattresses made from goose feathers. The bed factories are amazing!"

"Is Morocco a country, Princess?"

"Yes, Morocco is a country in the northern part of Africa."

I curtsied to her, thinking that she would make a wonderful queen someday. She smiled.

Suddenly, I thought of something. Maybe Zoerinda was the princess in the story in *The Princess and the Pea*. I hadn't thought about it before, but now it was clear. Zoerinda's story about her parents dying, growing up with her governess, meeting Jean, and being tested by the queen all pointed to one conclusion.

The facts all fit the story. I hadn't realized it before because, in the story, there was no sorcerer, no prediction of an attack, and no Berbers. At least in the story that I read.

If I was right, I bet the Queen forgot to take the pea out from under the princess's mattresses. That's why the princess slept so badly for years. Quickly, I suggested that the princess get down from her bed. She agreed. Then I took off the mattresses one by one. The princess stood by, confused. Arthur looked amused by this process and sighed with relief. Finally, I retrieved a pea, the size of a small stone, from the princess's bed. I handed it to the princess, smiling, "I think you will sleep better from now on."

Then I turned to Arthur, "Arthur, what do you think?"

The princess frowned when I called the bed Arthur, but when
he answered, she smiled. The princess had already learned at a
young age that things are not always as they seem.

Arthur was very firm in his answer. "I am the best bed in the
world!"

"Of course, you are," I said sweetly, "Do you know where they
manufacture the best beds in the world? The Berbers want to
settle in a new bed land. They want to live where the best beds
are made."

He said quickly, "You mean a homeland!"

I thought for a minute, "No, a bed land."

Arthur mulled this over a while, "I think that the princess is
right. A famous bed factory in Morocco built me."

"I will see you both later," I called over my shoulder and
hurried downstairs.

I found Saeed smoking a pipe, "I asked my friends, and I've
learned that Morocco has the best beds in the world."

Saeed demanded, "Are they bed experts?"

"Yes, they know a lot about beds."

"Thank you very much! Thank you! We will go to Morocco
and see the beds. Then, if your friends are right, we will have
found a home." He motioned to his men. Soon they galloped

away on their horses.

I ran back to Arthur. "The princess and the kingdom will be safe now. Saeed and the Berbers are leaving to go to Morocco."

"Who is Saeed?" Arthur demanded to know.

"He is the Berber chief. A chief is like a king or president."

"Are we safe," the princess demanded. "I heard the noise of the men and the horses. I was so scared that the sorcerer's prophecy had come true! Are they really leaving? So, they weren't looking to start a war?"

"No. No. They were never looking to start a war. They were only looking for a new home for their people. They were not looking to hurt anyone. They wanted a place where they could find good beds. So, I told them to go to Morocco like you both said, and they agreed."

"I did not think you could help. You are so young."

She stopped talking. She stared at me; her eyes full of admiration.

She took off an exquisite filigree gold necklace that she was wearing. She slipped the gold chain around my neck and said, "I want you to have this necklace. I would also like to make you a lady in waiting. You have shown great kindness and courage in helping me and my kingdom. If Jean were here, he might even make Arthur a knight. I am so sorry that I do not have that power. My kingdom thanks you both."

I smiled at the princess. "You're very welcome. People must help others. My mother taught me that. Saeed scared me at first, I admit, but I had to do everything needed to help you. I had to do my best. I am glad it was enough." I grinned a silly grin.

I turned to Arthur, "I'm getting a little tired," I admitted.

"Well, I should think so. You saved a princess and me too. You helped the Berbers find a new home, a bed land as you called it. Unfortunately, I think it's time to end this fairyland adventure."

KidQuest: Do you know how to curtsey or bow in case you meet a princess?

Now, let's finish the story.

Chapter 10
The Bedtime Stories Continue

When I woke the next day, I tried to explain to Mom and Dad about Princess Zoerinda, Arthur, and the Berbers. They smiled but were confused. So, after breakfast, I ran over to Mrs. G's house. We sat and talked for hours. I told Mrs. G the whole story. She laughed and laughed. She agreed it was a great first adventure with Arthur.

I thanked her for Arthur as I finally understood that Mrs. G had given me Arthur because I needed a friend. Then, we munched on chocolate chip cookies. We laughed about Arthur, the Princess, and the Berbers.

"How long will I have Arthur?" I finally asked, a bit concerned about what her answer would be.

"You will have him for all your bedtime stories." Then she grinned her funny, toothy, crooked smile.

I grinned back. I was so glad we moved to Treetown. I was delighted that Mrs. G was my first friend in town. I was happy that I had Arthur too. While Arthur and I are not exactly friends

despite Mrs. G's plan, Arthur and I are getting used to each other.
That's a good start. Isn't it? I can't wait for our next adventure.

THE END

KidQuest: Sorry that the adventure is over? See you soon for another adventure. Do you like circuses? Maybe we could go together.

JOIN US SOON FOR THE NEXT IN THE
ZOEY AND ARTHUR ADVENTURE
SERIES

The Great Bednapping Mystery

While Zoey and her family are on their first vacation in years, something tragic happens at home. Mrs. G and Zoey must help Arthur and some new friends who are in trouble. But how to help? Will Mrs. G's magical powers save the day, or must Zoey earn some new tricks to save the circus and Arthur?

Come join Zoey and me on our website,

www.joannahurleystories.com

What's in store for you there? Here are some of the things you will see:

Ask Zoey — Your kids can ask Zoey questions about anything — the story, their siblings, or any problems they have. I often take the feedback I hear from kids as inspiration for additional stories.

You can also find some of Zoey's favorite recipes on the website.

Parenting Quest You know it's hard being a parent. Whether it is work outside the home or in the house, life can be pretty demanding. Being a parent is a long-term quest. However, spending time with the kids should be and can be a joy. The goal with my books is to give you and your kids time to laugh, adventure together, and talk about important things like kindness, friendship, and courage. For parents, I have also provided free resources on instilling confidence, sibling bonding, teaching kindness, and more.

About the Author

Joanna Hurley is the pen name for Joanne Hurley. Joanna grew up in a small town in Michigan full of big personalities and small-town values. She was the second of seven children to a Spanish mother and Irish and English father. While her father did not feel that girls needed higher education, her mother convinced him to let Joanna go to university. She is still thankful for that opportunity.

Her mother taught her about hard work and doing her best. As a result, she chose law as a way to help people. Joanna worked for over 40 years as a business attorney. Working so closely with people taught Joanna about which strengths and weaknesses help people accomplish their goals or stood in their way.

Joanna used her knowledge about children and people when she started to write chapter books for children 6 to 11 years old. She loves the 6 - 11 age group because the kids are sassy, question everything, and are striving to become individuals. Joanna says she is still on that same quest and so relates.

Her stories are wacky and imaginative. The strong characters have traits like confidence and kindness, necessary for children to be happy now and later as adults. Joanna strongly believes that a lack of confidence is one thing that robs people of their ability to find happiness in life. Her writing and speaking engagements focus on these issues.

Joanna believes that she has retained the child she was at eight years old, a combination of Joan of Arc and bossy dragon slayer. Catch a glimpse of Joanna when she is writing, and she can be found laughing as she considers one crazy idea after another. Joanna loved reading as a child, feeling the excitement of each new story and wonderful illustrations. She thinks that books opened her world. Joanna currently explores the world from her home in the South of France.

Made in the USA
Monee, IL
21 October 2021